BOYS ARE SUPER STRONG!

Heroic Stories about Courage, Strength and Bravery - Present for Boys

Annabel E. Lewis

ISBN – 9798595445634

Table of Contents

This book belongs to

_____

Introduction
(For Parents)

Welcome to this beautiful collection of short stories.

I recently found myself unable to shake the thought that kids are hooked on technology. Phones, tablets, computers and consoles seem to dominate the minds of our kids. I say this after witnessing a very stressed-out looking mother soothing her child in the supermarket with an iPad. Still, maybe this isn't entirely the case.

After all, what do children these days *actually* want? Entertainment? Sure. Something to do? Of course. Yet, the more I thought about it, the more I realized that kids want just one thing. **Engaging stories**.

Sure, devices are engaging, but a true story from the heart that captures and bewilders a child can be just as compelling. Just as enthralling.

Just as life-changing.

Remember when you were a kid and were hooked on every word as your mother or father read to you in bed, or perhaps curled up on the sofa on a rainy Sunday afternoon? Do you remember the characters, the stories, and the worlds that you explored? Some of these have probably stayed with you your entire life, and it's something I want to bring back through this book.

And, of course, with an opportunity to share some captivating stories, I believe it would be such a shame not to include some rich lessons and fables that would help your children to see life in a new way, encouraging them to believe in themselves, to see life for the beautiful gift it is, to appreciate and feel grateful for their lives. All of these points can come together to help your kids grow up to become their best selves.

This is precisely what I've aimed to achieve within the pages of this book.

These stories are bold, imaginative, and beautiful. Some are original, others inspired by some of the greatest short stories and moral examples of our times, all adapted for your children to read with you, on their own, or with their friends.

Testing some of these stories out with my own kids, I've now got some amazing photos to remember when we all dressed up and acted out the stories. It was an afternoon I'll never forget.

I can't stress how incredible a good story can be, both reading them and creating them yourself. Isn't it just amazing how words on a page can say so much and create such vibrant and vivid images that can change the way we live our lives for the better?

Just as a final note before jumping in, if you enjoy reading these stories, then it would mean the absolute world to me if you're able to take the time to leave a review wherever you purchased this book. I always find it so amazing to read through your comments and reviews, and I love hearing feedback from you.

This also inspires me to keep writing and producing more books. It makes me happy to hear that you're happy, so please, leave me a few words. I'm excited to hear from you.

Okay, that's enough from me. Let's get straight into these stunning adventures. Grab your duvet. Wrap up warm. Get in bed or on the sofa. Turn the lights down. Reading glasses, anyone? Let's go.

Story One – The Boy Who Dreamed Bigger Than Ever

Kyle was just an average boy, and he knew it. Every day in his life felt the same. He would go to school and come home again. He would watch the same television shows, hang out with the same friends, and play in the same parks.

Not that Kyle thought there was anything wrong with his life. He was actually really rather happy. He got good grades at school. His friends were nice and made him laugh, and the park had the best grass for playing football on. It always seemed to be sunny in that park.

Yet, Kyle had one thing in his life that excited him more than anything in the world. Whenever the weekend arrived, this one thing got him so excited, he couldn't help but bounce around all over the house until his mother or father would take him to play.

Play what, you ask? Well, Kyle loved to play tennis.

Kyle could never quite put his finger on what he loved so much about tennis. Was it how hard he could hit the ball and how fast he could make it fly over the net? Was it running forwards and backwards so fast, putting in all his energy into winning, and then scoring that well-earned point? Was it the lovely boys and girls he played with at the tennis club? Kyle thought it was probably all of those things and more. Whatever the reason, Kyle knew that tennis made him happier than anything else.

His love for tennis started when he was only a small boy. Kyle's father would take him to play at his club's tennis courts every single weekend. When Kyle moved up to the higher schools, they had their own tennis courts, so he started playing every single break time and joined the tennis club.

Even when it was raining or the tennis club wasn't on one day, Kyle would endlessly watch tennis matches on television. He would follow all the competitions from around the world and knew all the best players' names. Kyle dreamed that, one day, maybe people would know his name in the same way as well.

As Kyle grew up, this dream was something he started to take more and more seriously. When he got home from school, he would rush through all his homework just so he could hit the tennis ball against the wall of his house. He hoped to get better so that, one day, he could play with the professionals.

In fact, Kyle started taking his dream so seriously that he would even hit the ball against the walls at school during his break time. But only when the tennis clubs weren't on, of course.

However, Kyle didn't do this without the other kids noticing.

"Haha!" the other kids laughed. "Look at Kyle. He's playing with the ball all by himself. Don't you have any friends to play with, Kyle?"

Kyle's spirits sank and he couldn't hide how sad the comments made him feel.

One day, the other kids were so mean, they teased Kyle all day. He just wanted to get better at playing tennis. That was it. So he went home and told his parents what was happening.

"Mom, I don't know what to do," Kyle said at dinner. "All the kids are being mean to me, but all I am doing is playing the game I love so much. Maybe I should stop and play football with the rest of the kids. Would they still pick on me then?"

Kyle's mother was very wise. She had once been a child who had been picked on by others.

"Remember, Kyle," his mother said, stroking his head softly with her hand, as she always did, "if you are passionate about playing tennis and you are really doing what you love, then you don't need to listen to what anybody else says. Yes, what they are saying is mean, but you need to do what you need to do."

Kyle agreed and knew his mother was right. While it was hard to deal with all the horrible comments, he still knew, deep down in his gut, that he was doing what he loved, and he couldn't stop just because of the things other people said. He could never give up doing the one thing he loved more than anything in the world.

And so, he didn't.

One day, Kyle's mother noticed a tennis competition was being held in the next town. Kyle was so excited about the idea of playing in a real competition that his mother signed him up. Kyle would be playing his first game in two weeks.

He practiced every single day, and when the big day arrived, Kyle knew he was ready.

His mother and father drove him to the next town. When they arrived at the competition, Kyle noticed he was the youngest player there. Everyone else seemed much older, taller, and stronger than he was. He tightened his grip on his racket. He felt very nervous, but he didn't want this to put him off.

"I'm going to do this. I am playing the game I love," he told himself sternly.

After signing in, Kyle played his first game. Then he played his second. Then his third. He won every game.

Kyle was nervous. By the middle of the day, there were more people in the crowd than he had ever seen. This was scary, but he didn't let their screams and shouts put him off. He was here to do what he loved, and nobody could say anything about it.

Kyle played more games and continued to win each one. By the end of the afternoon, he realized he had beaten everyone and had made it through to the final round. Nervous but excited, he faced the last player. After a nail-biting game that

Kyle put absolutely everything he had to give into, he won the cup and the prize money!

Everybody in the crowd clapped and cheered for Kyle because of his amazing performance. He had done so well, beating every single player in the competition. Even the local newspaper came to ask him some questions and take his photograph. Within a week, everybody at school knew what Kyle had achieved.

They all praised him for winning and thought that what he had done was amazing.

But still, just like Kyle chose not to care what people thought when they teased him, he decided not to care what they thought about him winning.

Kyle knew that through hard work and determination, he was able to keep doing what he loved. To him, that was all that mattered, no matter what other people thought or said.

Story Two – The Old Man and the Cave

A long time ago, in a faraway land, an old man called Mark lived in the hollow of a hill, not far from a small village in a valley below.

Mark lived off the land; his breakfast was mushrooms, and his dinner, bark stew. The villagers laughed hard when they saw him, and playfully called him Mad Mark. For who would eat bark when there was plenty of lamb?

But Mark didn't mind, he didn't want all those friends. No nagging or bragging, that's what people did. No point in pretending he cared for their natter.

This gave him more time to do what he wanted. Mark loved to find treasures by the stream down below. The water washed up great things the villagers had lost. A brass trinket here, and a gold coin over there. With no names attached, Mark could take them all home.

In no time at all, his cave brimmed over with things he had found. Mark was sure of two things. His cave was his fortress, his treasure was safe. The other was sad but as true as could be. Because they didn't like him, the villagers would never come calling.

Which was why on that faithful spring evening, Mark was shocked to come home to find not just one, but all the villagers at the mouth of his cave.

"What brings you all here?" he asked with a frown.

The people looked around, not sure how to start.

"A big storm is coming, we need a safe place to shelter. The river will rise and flood all our homes. We'll share what we have if you'll let us come in."

Mark looked up above. They had a fair point. From nowhere at all, the sky had grown dark and a wind had come fast.

He thought of his cave and all that he had. His home was quite large, but it was filled with his trove. To let just one in, he'd have to throw out his gold. If he gave up his treasure, would he ever get it back?

"There's room for one," he said with a sigh, "but that's all I've got." If he threw out some shoes, he could live with the loss.

The villagers looked quite aghast.

"We are a hundred at least, there must be more room. If you leave us out here, we'll lose more than gold."

Mark looked from left to right, then to the front and behind him. Children cried loudly as mothers held on tightly. Men wrung their hats as they waited in fright. All those who had jeered and called him Mad Mark were now at his mercy. He could do as he liked.

A rain drop fell down, they were now out of time. Mark shook his head and waved at the crowd.

"You'll all have to help, we have no time at all."

The villagers all sighed and some followed him in. They gasped as they saw all that Mark had amassed. A mother's brass trinket here, and a trader's gold coin over there. The people were shocked to see all of their stuff. But Mark was right, they had no time at all.

They worked really fast to move it all out, every last trinket and every last coin. As Mark's treasures grew less and the people piled in, he tried not to think of all of his toil.

The rain fell down hard for hours on end. They waited and listened as the gale battered the door. Close to dusk, just as babies were yawning, the wind grew less fierce, and all was at rest.

The people all cheered and thanked their Mad Mark. No life had been lost, and all had been spared. They all trooped back home, dancing merrily with glee.

When he found himself alone, Mark stood in his cave and looked around. He'd lost all his treasure, not a single thing was left. He wailed in the corner and mourned his great loss. It could take a lifetime to recover, and he might never find it all.

A day went past, Mark sat still in a state. He thought of all the things he had stored in his cave. From nowhere at all, a knock came at the door. Mark looked quite confused. Guests two days in a row?

He opened the door, all ready to shout. A girl stood outside, her mother beside her. And in her hand, she held a box of bright colored buttons.

"This is my stash, I know it's not gold, but it's something I treasure. I'd like you to have it, to say thanks for your kindness. We all heard you crying, I hope you feel better."

Mark smiled at the girl and asked them in for tea. Now he had no more treasure, he had room for the guests.

Just as they were seated, another knock sounded. Mark raised his head swiftly, quite sure he'd misheard. But a boy stood out there with his big brother behind him.

"I know it's not treasure, but I've brought you some bark. I heard you like stew which is made from this tree."

Mad Mark felt a warm glow fill up his tight chest, but it wasn't from the buttons or the bark for the stew. The love from the children was filling his cave up. And so Mark let them in, and the next group behind them. The people kept coming with trickles of kindness.

In no time at all, Mark's cave was brimming. Not with brass trinkets or gold coins, but with the warmth of laughter and friendship. For the one thing Mad Mark hadn't quite wanted, had turned out to be just what he had needed.

Story Three – The Problem Breakfast

There once lived a boy called Malcolm. He had a bit of a problem.

No matter what happened, Malcolm seemed to always find that he felt sad about his life, but he couldn't quite put his finger on why.

People told him, "You can't always be happy. Everybody feels sad from time to time. It's just a natural part of life."

While Malcolm accepted this, the main problem was that he felt as though he had nothing to be happy for. His grades weren't very good, and all his friends from school were interested in playing sports and video games, but Malcolm didn't like doing any of these things.

Instead, Malcolm enjoyed reading, but it made him feel very lonely to read all day by himself while all the other kids played outside together.

One morning, Malcolm went downstairs for breakfast, and his father was already sitting at the table. Malcolm sat next to him and started talking to his dad about how he felt.

Malcolm's father listened to him and hoped more than anything there was a way he could make him feel better. It was at this moment that his father suddenly had an idea.

He stood up and went over to the kitchen cupboard to grab a few items, and then came back with three things that he placed on the table: a potato, a handful of coffee beans, and an egg.

"Now, son, tell me, what do you see here?" his father asked.

Malcolm looked at the items for a moment, trying to see whether something was wrong with the food or if his father was asking him a trick question.

"I see a potato, an egg and some coffee beans. Nothing special."

"Okay," his father replied, "do you want to eat any of these for breakfast? Without me cooking them first?"

"Eww," said Malcolm. "No! The egg is raw and gross. The potato is cold and hard. And the coffee beans are just coffee beans. I can't drink or eat any of it."

"Agreed," said his father. "Now give me a moment."

His father then picked up the ingredients, went to the kitchen counter, and started cooking. About twenty minutes passed before he returned to the table with a plate of lovely, cooked food.

"Now," said Malcolm's father, "tell me what you see."

"Well, now the food's cooked, of course I would eat it," Malcolm said, his mouth watering. His father had even added a few sausages. "The coffee has the best coffee smell, the egg is cooked just the way I like it, and the potato is mashed up, hot, and ready to eat. Is this my breakfast?"

His father laughed. "You see, son, imagine all these ingredients are the problems in your life. When you first saw them, you didn't want anything because they were all raw and uncooked. Understandable. However, once you work on them, in this case cooking them and preparing the food to eat, suddenly, what you thought was a problem at the beginning turned out to be something beautiful and tasty! You just have to put the work in."

The boy thought about his father's advice for a moment and realized what he said was right. Perhaps his problems weren't problems at all, but simply ingredients he could turn into something beautiful.

Story Four – The Silent Princess

In the kingdom of Essa, where magic still ruled the land, an old mage called Mica was called to the palace to meet with the prince. Mica was worried, for everyone knew the prince was a bully and his temper was short.

The mage bowed low when he stood before His Highness. The prince was unsmiling, in fact, he looked rather cross. Mica was sure he would kick up a fuss.

"I have a great problem I need you to solve," the prince wasted no time in stating his case.

Mica bowed lower and said in a voice filled with caution, "Of course, Your Highness, I'll do whatever I can."

"I met a princess on one of my travels. She's kind and she's gentle, but she won't say a word. I'm sure with your magic you'll be able to put things right."

Mica thought hard, but knew this was tricky. His magic was strong, but he could not loosen a tongue.

"Have you tried a doctor," Mica dared to ask, for it sounded like that's what the princess required.

But the prince got mad and stomped his foot hard. "I know what she needs, some magic should help."

Mica thought not, but knew he should try, if only to show the prince he was wrong.

They went to the princess who sat in a room. The curtains were closed and she looked rather drawn. She sighed as they entered, and turned to the wall. She held both her cheeks in the palms of her hands.

Mica raised his arms high and conjured a spell. It was one he knew well and he liked it a lot. The room filled with smoke and blinded them all, but Mica formed a clear bubble around himself and the princess.

"Your Highness, I'd rather you showed me what's causing the fuss."

The princess was surprised, for no one else had bothered to ask what the problem was. She let her hands drop, so the mage could see what was wrong. He nodded as the princess gestured and pointed. When all the smoke cleared, Mica now knew what had to be done.

He asked the young prince to grant him one tiny request.

"My magic will work but only with this one small thing. I have a dear friend who knows some magic as well. She'll be here in no time and all will be well."

Mica's friend arrived with a black bag in her hand. She pulled out some forceps and put on her gloves.

"We call this dental magic, it's all the rave now," Mica explained to the prince when he started to rant.

The dentist reached inside the princess's mouth, and very gently pulled out two large wisdom teeth. It turned out the princess had been in great pain, but now she could talk and she could laugh with the prince.

And what we have learned from this really quick tale is, sometimes it is best if we ask people questions before we take charge and go off making blunders.

Story Five – Karma of the Birds and the Bees

In the heart of a beautiful woodland, somewhere hidden deep in the world, there was a gigantic tree that grew on the edge of a river. Here, many of the animals who lived across the land would gather to drink and bathe in the water.

It was inside this big, tall tree that a family of bees decided to build their home. It took several weeks, but eventually the beehive was finished, and the bees were so happy to call this place their new home.

Every day, the bees would fly to and from the beehive, visiting all the nearby flowers and bushes to collect pollen so that they could make their sweet, delicious honey.

One day, during the hottest summer the woodland had seen for many, many years, a single bee flew down to the edge of the river to get a drink. However, as the bee arrived, a sudden gust of wind blew it into the water before it had even taken its first sip!

The bee struggled and soon realized it wasn't strong enough to get back out again.

From high above the river, in another tree, a sparrow had been lazily watching the bee and saw it fall into the flowing water of the river. Full of empathy and compassion, full of love, the sparrow quickly flew down from the branches of the tree, grabbing a leaf from a branch on the way down.

Very carefully, the sparrow landed ahead of the bee and placed the leaf on the surface of the water, and with a sudden motion, safely scooped the bee up and out of the water.

The sparrow picked up the leaf and carried it over to the shore. The bee sputtered and coughed up some water, still feeling very shocked and confused about everything that had just happened.

"Thank you so much," the bee said gratefully. "You saved my life. How can I repay you?"

"Think nothing of it," the sparrow replied and flew off back to his tree.

A few weeks later, the bee was living another day, much like every other day. He woke up and flew out of the hive for another day of collecting pollen to make sweet honey. The bee flew over the river towards the flower bushes on the other side but soon noticed a lot of noise coming from behind some of the trees. Curious, the little bee flew over to see what was happening.

As soon as the trees parted, the bee saw the same sparrow that saved him all those weeks ago, hiding behind a large rock. The sparrow was scared, so scared, as a huge cat swiped through the air with its paws trying to catch it. The bee rushed over to the rescue.

Using all of his strength, the bee flew straight towards the cat as fast as he could and stung the cat with his stinger, right on his back!

The cat meowed so loudly in shock, completely stunned by the sudden pain and swelling on its back. Almost straight away, he forgot all about the sparrow and ran off into the woods.

Realizing the cat was gone, the sparrow turned and saw the bee, sitting on a nearby flower smiling at him.

"Thank you so much," the sparrow said. "You have indeed saved my life."

"Not a problem," the bee said. "If you do good things for others, good things will always happen to you. It's the law of karma!"

Story Six — The $20 Note

Once, there was a city with a school. The school was just like any school you would find anywhere else in the world, and the teachers who worked in the school were all very passionate about teaching their students. However, our story focuses on one teacher in particular who goes by the name of Mr. Johnson.

Mr. Johnson noticed something in all his classes. It didn't matter if they were smart, or good at sports, or even just nice people, his students didn't seem to have any confidence in themselves. They would always put themselves down or call themselves dumb if they got a question wrong, even if they weren't actually dumb.

Mr. Johnson took it upon himself to teach the kids that they are valuable and beautiful, and mean something in this world. And so, Mr. Johnson came up with an idea.

During one lesson, Mr. Johnson stood up at the front of the class and pulled out a brand-new $20 note which he took out of the bank earlier that morning. He held it up to the class, showing them all clearly what it was.

The eyes of the students lit up. $20 was a lot of money, and it was clear that something was about to happen with it. Perhaps one of them was going to get the note for themselves, many of the students thought.

"Who, out of anybody in this class, wants this $20 note?" Mr. Johnson asked.

Every student in the class shot their hands into the air, eager to get the $20 note.

"But wait," said the teacher. He then took the $20 note and screwed it all up into a little ball in his hand. When the teacher opened his fist, the note was crinkled and wasn't anywhere near as nice as it had just looked.

"Even after I have screwed the note up," Mr. Johnson said, "who still wants me to give them this $20 note?"

Again, the students' hands all shot up into the air. The teacher smiled to himself. Then, instead of choosing a student to give the note to, he threw it down onto the ground and stamped on it several times with his foot, rubbing his boot across it and twisting it into the ground.

"Now, who, after I've screwed this $20 note up and stamped it into the ground, still wants this $20 note?"

Again, without any hesitation, the students all put their hands in the air.

"You see, my students," Mr. Johnson said wisely, "just like the $20 note I have here, it doesn't matter whether I screw it up, stamp on it, or make it anything other than its pristine self, the value of the $20 note remains the same."

"This same lesson applies to you and your own life. It doesn't matter what hardships or trials you go through or find yourself in. It doesn't matter how many things you get wrong or how far away from perfect you feel. You still hold the same amount of value, no matter what.

Story Seven — Stinky Jeremy

Jeremy Hubble stank badly, just like a skunk who'd run amok. He smelled so vile, even his shadow shrank back. For that's how you get when you don't take a bath.

His poor mother had tried to get him to wash, but Jeremy yelled and fought like a bull.

"I don't see the point when I'll just get dirty again?"

His mother screamed high, his father just sighed. The days went by and the boy held his own. Before they all knew it, a whole month had gone.

His friends held their noses, his teachers were shocked, but Jeremy just wouldn't get in the tub.

Springtime was looming, the flowers were blooming, and everyone longed to smell the roses and lilies. Bright petals of red and blooms of pale orange, they all smiled with joy at the thought of the sight.

They gathered at Hope Park, all ready for sniffing, but Jeremy came running and blew through the bushes.

The townsfolk were livid. They covered their faces, for Jeremy's stench had put off all of the lilies. Instead of sweet fragrance, all they got was his foul scent.

The people all roared and marched to his home.

"It's now quite disturbing, something's got to be done," they said to his parents when they opened the door.

His mother was crying, his father just frowned. But Jeremy laughed hard and slithered away.

They called a town meeting to hatch a plan, for everyone was fed up of one little boy. The people talked high, the people talked low, yet no one could come up with anything good.

But just as it was starting to look like a bust, a young man stood up and took to the floor. They all knew him well, he was the town's clown. He showed up at birthdays and made the kids smile.

"I know a neat trick to get him to wash," the young man declared, and he told them his plan.

That evening, as Jeremy raced through the town, spreading his pong as he knocked all about, a group waited patiently just outside his house.

When he turned a sharp corner and saw them all gathered, he spun right around to flee from their clutches. Another group sprang out from where he had turned.

The young clown was there and he held a small jar.

"I'm sorry to do this, but you leave us no choice." Then the clown poured itching powder all down Jeremy's back.

The powder was working, it started to sting. Jeremy ran home like the wind as he felt the first itch. He reached for his back, his body was prickly. But try as he may, he couldn't quite reach the itch.

"A shower will help take the itching away." His mother was smiling, she had the tub filled.

Young Jeremy had no choice but to dive in to wash. The water worked well, and the soap even better. And when he was done, he smelt just like candy.

The townsfolk all cheered when he opened the door. His face was all shiny, and his smell no more sour.

"Just you wait," Jeremy cried as he walked through the park, "tomorrow I'll start to smell awful again."

But the people all smiled as they showed him their purses. They all held small jars to be at the ready.

All month long, the townsfolk were always on guard. When they saw Stinky Jeremy, they shook their bulging purses and smiled.

At last, Jeremy grew tired of hiding in corners. He longed once again to be out with the others, for even his friends had been armed with the powder.

And so, he decided to give baths a chance. Just once every day like his mother had asked.

The townsfolk were happy, the air smelt like roses, and everyone could finally enjoy the bright orange lilies.

But if you looked closely, even after months had passed, you'd see a small lump in all of their purses. This was just to make sure Stinky Jeremy never came back.

Story Eight – The Boy Who Visited the Circus

Sam had one dream when he was growing up as a child, and that dream was to visit the circus. After seeing shows on television, he wanted nothing more than to see one in real life with his own eyes. So, when he was just seven years old, his parents decided to take him for his birthday, and he had never been so happy.

What made Sam even happier was that he would see one of the most amazing and most fantastic circuses in the world. He couldn't believe they were actually coming to his hometown!

When Sam's birthday arrived, he put on his best clothes, then made sure he went to the toilet and wasn't hungry or thirsty before he left. He didn't want to miss a single moment of the show.

Sam, his mother, and father, and even his sister, Scarlet, got in the car and left for the circus grounds. When they arrived at the local park where the circus was being held, the boy's eyes lit up in wonder and excitement.

Cars were arriving from all directions. Groups of people, families, and friends were huddled around, making their way up a long grass track towards the biggest tent Sam had ever seen. It was huge, with massive red and white strips going all the way along the side.

Everything looked so beautiful. The lights from inside the tent were glowing like candles in the dark. Sam and his family followed the crowd up the grass path towards the tent, which only seemed to become bigger with every step.

As they arrived at the tent's entrance, the crowd was starting to fill out with odd-looking characters. A man on stilts walked past, towering over everyone, looking down on the people to wave while smiling at them. Off to one side, another man was juggling balls that were actually on fire. A girl Sam thought was really pretty, had a beard growing all the way down to the ground and around her legs. Her beard even had a monkey sitting on the end!

Sam inhaled all the sweets and candy smells wafting through the air as the crowd moved forward again. He heard children laughing, and parents talking. Some people had candy floss on sticks, and others had ice cream. Sam couldn't wait to have some of his own as his birthday treat.

Everyone bought tickets and found their seats inside the massive tent. After a few minutes, and after making sure everyone was sitting down, the lights dimmed, and the show began.

The show was even better than Sam could ever have imagined. Some performers walked high up in the air on the thinnest ropes. Others swung from one side of the tent to the other, flipping through the air as they went. Other people guided lions to jump through flaming hoops. One man even juggled chainsaws with shiny, sharp blades!

However, Sam's favorite act in the show was the elephants. Sam had never seen an animal so big or so strong, and the way they moved together made Sam's eyes fill with awe.

Sam was so captivated by the elephants, he couldn't think about any of the other acts that appeared in the show. When the first half of the show finally ended, the boy was eager for more. He and his father wandered off to have a look around the grounds, getting themselves some fresh air.

After wandering around for a few minutes, watching some of the other acts getting ready for the second half, they suddenly came across a rather quiet tent. The door was open, and peering inside, Sam and his father saw the three giant elephants from the show. They were still just as beautiful.

"Wow," Sam said. "They are the most amazing animals I've ever seen."

His father agreed.

Sam stood in awe and watched for a moment. Then a thought suddenly occurred to him.

Why would the elephants stand there in the tent if they could be free to go wherever they wanted? They were so big and could easily just run away if they wanted to. He looked closer. He saw a piece of thin rope around each elephant's leg that tied the elephants to a small wooden stake in the ground.

This made Sam laugh to himself.

"What's so funny?" his father asked.

"Why do the elephants stay here when they could be free to go wherever they want? They are tied up with rope, but they could easily break free. They are massive animals, and the rope is only thin and could break so easily."

His father thought for a moment.

"You're right," he finally said. "The elephants could break free at any time they want. They are far stronger than any other animal or person in this entire circus. However, when the elephants were small, maybe about the same size as you, they were tied up by the same rope, but they were too small to move it. As they've grown up, they don't believe they have become stronger, so they still believe the rope is holding them in place. Basically, they have given up trying to break free."

"The elephants have stopped believing in themselves?"

"That's right," his father replied. "If they kept trying to break free every day, then they would have easily escaped when they grew big enough, but they didn't. They gave up when they couldn't do it and then lost whatever belief they had in themselves. There's a good lesson to be learned there."

"What lesson?"

"If you want something in life, something you want more than anything else, you should never give up fighting for it. The thing is, even if you're not able to do it right now, that doesn't mean you won't be able to do it in the future. So, don't give up!"

Sam took his father's advice on board and decided from that moment on, he was never going to give up on anything he set out to achieve.

Story Nine – The Butterfly Freed

There once was a man who loved to tend to his garden. In fact, the man put so many hours into his garden, it was easily the most beautiful garden for miles around. Every single day, he would have breakfast and spend every moment until dinner time there. He would do all the jobs like pulling up all the weeds and pruning the plants and flowers. He made sure the grass was cut to the perfect length and even made little homes for all the animals, like the hedgehogs and the birds, to live in.

One morning, he was sat in his little chair that overlooked his garden, simply enjoying the view of everything he had created. It was all so beautiful. Then he decided to go for a little walk around.

As he passed the flower beds, he saw the roses and the sunflowers. He stopped to take photos of them, sniffing their wonderful smells, and seeing such pretty details on their petals. He couldn't help but pull out a few small weeds as he went.

At the end of his garden, he went down to the small pond to see the fishes he kept there. He saw the frogs and the fishes playing together, the frogs on the lily pads hopping from one to the other, a fish jumping as it tried to catch a bug that flew too close to the water.

It was here, while he was admiring the pond, that he noticed something strange stuck to the branches of one of the nearby trees. He walked over slowly to inspect it. It took a little while, but the man eventually realized that what he was looking at was the cocoon of a tiny little butterfly.

Wow, he thought to himself. He had never seen a butterfly cocoon before. He admired it for a while, before carrying on with his day. That night, he dreamed of the butterfly emerging. It was so royal and elegant, so beautiful. When the man awoke, he vowed that all he wanted was to see the beautiful butterfly emerge.

And so, every day, he made his way down to the pond to watch the cocoon, waiting for the exact moment in which it would open to reveal the beautiful butterfly inside.

Soon a month had passed, and while the little cocoon had started to move from time to time, and even while the man knew the cocoon would soon be open, he couldn't wait any longer. There was no sign of the butterfly, and the man's patience had run out.

One morning, he decided enough was enough. He had breakfast, threw open the door, stormed down to the pond at the bottom of the garden with a pair of scissors, and waited for the butterfly cocoon to move. When it didn't, because of course it wasn't ready, he carefully slipped the scissors into the side of the cocoon.

"Don't worry, little butterfly," he said out loud, but unsure whether the butterfly would hear him. "I'm here to set you free."

And with that, the man took the scissors and ever so slowly and gently slipped the blade into the outer layer of the cocoon and began to cut. The man was very gentle and careful because, of course, he didn't want to cut the butterfly. Easily enough, the butterfly was set free of the cocoon, and tried to stretch open its new, beautiful wings for the first time.

But something wasn't right.

The butterfly wasn't ready to come out of its cocoon and wasn't strong enough to be free. Instead of being a beautiful butterfly, all the cocoon held was a little soft caterpillar body with wings so weak, they looked just like water and simply fell to nothing.

Once again, the butterfly tried to spread its wings out and even tried to fly, but there was nothing to fly with. With no strength, the butterfly rolled off the branch into the pond below, drifted away with the flowing water, and was gone forever.

The man felt very guilty about what he had done and had learned a very powerful lesson. Beautiful things take time to grow, and everybody needs to be patient until this happens. The tallest, most beautiful trees in the world must first dig deep into the ground to grow their roots, so they can survive the harshest storms.

In the same way, a butterfly must go through months of being in a cocoon on its own, growing and developing, before it can become the beautiful butterfly it was born to be.

Story Ten – The Treasure Fields

In a faraway land, there was a quiet village on the edge of a quiet city. Here, you would find beautiful countryside that stretches as far as the eye could see. This was a place where birds sang in the trees from morning until night, children ran around barefoot in the street, and the air was filled with amazing smells from the fields and bakeries.

It was here, in this little village, there lived a farmer who worked very hard to provide for his family and ensure his farm was a successful one. Every year, the farmer would grow different crops on the land. One year he grew corn, and the next he grew grain. Then he grew grapes, and when the hottest year ever came around, he even managed to grow cocoa beans to make chocolate.

The farmer worked very hard for his entire life to help this family, which included his wife and two sons. While the farmer worked hard on the land, his wife stayed at home to look after the house and to raise the children as best she could.

Alas, while they had hardworking parents, the two sons didn't see the value of hard work. They never knew what it was like to be poor and to be without money. They thought that everything was just fine all the time, not realizing their parent's work made it all possible. Instead of working, they would sit around the garden all day and chose not to work in the fields with their father. That seemed like too much hard work for no reason.

Time passed, and the farmer became older and older until he one day realized he was very ill and unable to work anymore.

Fearing for his life, the farmer was worried about who was going to look after the family, and who was going to look after the farm. Without the farm, there would be no money to live. The boys didn't know how to work on the farm and had no motivation to do so.

So, as the farmer felt his death was approaching, he came up with a plan.

One day, when the sons went to visit their father in the hospital, he told them to come close so that he could tell them a secret.

"My sons, all these years, you haven't wondered how I made the money to keep the house running and to give you the best life possible. It is now I am going to tell you."

The boys leaned in closer to their father, eager to hear what he was about to say.

"Underneath my field, you can find buried treasure that is worth a fortune. It's a treasure that will keep your family safe and happy for many years to come."

The boys' eyes lit up with the idea of treasure, and since their father was too ill to show them where it was, they knew they would be able to search for it.

The tragic day arrived when the farmer passed away, and the boys were given the farm as their inheritance. Eager to see the treasure that their father had left them, the boys set off into the farm to try and dig it up.

Of course, the farm was massive and stretched across many fields, and while the boys worked hard every day to dig up the ground, it took months to dig up the entire place. Still, by the end of it all, they found no treasure.

One day, the sons noticed something. While no treasure or gold had been discovered, the act of digging up the ground ensured that all the seeds had turned over. This meant that beautiful, healthy crops had started to grow in the fields, and the family had another year of harvest to live on.

The sons recognized that their hard work of digging up the fields had produced the crops and therefore the money to live on. At last, they realized that the value of hard work was perhaps the best treasure their father could have given them.

Story Eleven – The Donkey in the Pit

This tale begins on the side of a cliff where there once was a farm. The farm was like any normal farm you would see in today's world. There were fields with crops and grains growing within their boundaries and a barn filled with all kinds of farmyard animals, including pigs, cows, and horses.

The farmer who owned the land lived a happy and simple life with his family. Farming was his passion, and he was living a life he loved. Despite all his horses, sheep, and cows, the farmer's favorite animal was his donkey.

Every year, the donkey helped transport goods to the markets and helped pull the plow through the fields. In the summer, the donkey and the farmer would even go to the beach to give children rides up and down the pier.

One day, while the farmer was working with the donkey in the field, the donkey rode a little too close to the edge of the cliff and ended up slipping and falling down the side. Shocked and afraid, the farmer ran over to the cliff edge and looked down. The donkey had rolled a little further and had fallen into a small pit. Small, yet too high for the donkey to simply climb out from.

The farmer ran back to the barns and grabbed the longest rope he could find before sprinting back to the cliff. He then chucked the rope down the hole desperately. But, of course, the donkey didn't know why. The farmer was in despair. If only the donkey had hands to grab the rope and get pulled up.

The farmer tried all day and all night to figure out the best way to get his favorite donkey out of the pit, but there were no options. Finally, after speaking with his family, the farmer decided it was time to put the donkey out of its misery and bury it. That would be far nicer than waiting for it to starve or dehydrate.

The next day, the farmer took a shovel and started to dig, chucking shovel after shovel of dirt off the cliff and into the pit. The farmer felt so sad and didn't dare look into the pit to see what was happening with the donkey. However, after an hour of digging, he found he couldn't resist looking down.

The sight was one he didn't expect to see.

With every shovel of dirt that had been thrown, the soil had hit the donkey's back. Without even thinking, the donkey had shaken the dirt from his body, causing it to fall to the ground where it was starting to pile up. Instead of being buried, the floor of the pit was slowly getting higher and higher!

The farmer was filled with sudden hope.

He dug faster and faster, pouring more dirt into the pit. He even called his family to grab a shovel and help. After just a few hours, the pit had filled up with so much dirt that it was no longer a pit but simply a flat piece of ground. The donkey was now able to take a step out of the pit and back onto solid ground.

The farmer then took the rope and lowered his son down the cliff edge. The boy tied the rope around the donkey, and within a few minutes, the donkey was pulled back up to safety.

From that day onwards, the farmer realized that there was no problem in life that couldn't be solved with a bit of hard work and creative thinking. He vowed to always think outside the box and face all his hardships and problems. He also built a fence around the cliff, so the donkey could never fall again.

Story Twelve – The Boy and the Nailed Fence

There once lived a boy called Alfie who had one of the worst tempers you could ever imagine. No matter what happened in life, Alfie would flip out and start shouting and crying as loud as he could. It doesn't matter if he dropped a pencil or if his shoelaces came untied.

For some reason, everything in life just made him so angry all the time.

Alfie was seriously struggling, and even though he wanted to, he didn't know how to make things better or how to stay calm. It just seemed impossible to stay relaxed. Thankfully, one day, after many years of feeling angry, Alfie's father came up with an idea.

Alfie's father took him outside and showed him the fence at the bottom of the garden. It was a regular wooden fence, but Alfie had never really paid too much attention to it.

"My son," Alfie's father said, "you don't want to go through life being an angry person, do you?

"No, father," he replied, "but I can't help it. I just get so angry."

"Well, I have a plan. I am giving you this fence to help you stay calm and to deal with your anger."

Alfie didn't feel very excited about getting a fence as a present, but he continued to listen to his father's plan.

"Now, my idea is very simple. Every time you feel yourself getting angry, all you need to do is come down here, pick up the nail and the hammer, and then bang the nail into the wood. With any luck, you won't feel angry after doing this!"

Alfie didn't really see why he was being asked to do this, but he decided to agree with his father and just see what happened. Of course, it didn't take long for Alfie to find himself getting angry again.

After going back inside the house, he found his little sister playing on the games console, meaning he couldn't have a go. Alfie wanted to play so badly and started to get so angry that he shouted and screamed and made all the fuss in the world.

His father quickly came over and reminded Alfie to go outside and take out his anger on the fence. That is what Alfie did. Over the next twenty-four hours, Alfie managed to bang forty-two nails into the fence. His father came out, looking shocked that there had been so many times the boy had been angry during just one day.

However, Alfie's father's plan didn't end there. Over the next month, Alfie would get angry, then go outside and hit more nails into the fence. When he came back, he would be nice and calm again. Slowly but surely, Alfie started to control his temper, and everyone saw how much of a difference it made. Even Alfie felt happier.

Eventually, after many months of banging in nails, Alfie was finally able to control his temper, and he didn't end up getting angry at everything all the time. But again, Alfie's father had another lesson to teach him.

One summer afternoon, Alfie and his father went back down to look at the fence at the bottom of the garden, which was now so full of nails, you could barely see any wood.

"Now Alfie," his father said, "I want you to try something new. Every time you're able to control your anger and stay calm, I want you to come down here and pull a nail out of the fence until every single nail is gone. Can you do this for me?"

"I can," Alfie replied.

And so, he did.

Every day that passed where the boy didn't lose his temper, which was nearly every single day, he would walk down to the bottom of the garden and pull a nail out of the fence. It took a few months, but eventually, every single nail was gone.

"Well done, my son," the father said to his boy. "I am very proud of you and how far you have come. It's amazing how far a little bit of effort goes."

The boy smiled at his father, happy with how proud he was of him, and how proud he was of himself.

"However, I want to show you something," his father went on.

They walked down to the fence one last time. His father pointed at the holes in the fence that had been left by the many hundreds of nails which had gone into the fence over the last few months and had just been taken out.

"As you can see," his father said, "the holes remain in the fence. This is a very important lesson to learn. Through anger and pain and sadness, you can act out and stick the nails into a fence, but there will always be a mark of what you did. A hole. A scar. Even if you accidentally break a plate from the kitchen and even if you glue it back together, the cracks from breaking the plate will always remain. It's the same with how you act."

"Sometimes," he said, "it doesn't matter how many times you say sorry, the wound will always still be there."

And with that, Alfie made sure that from that moment on, he was always careful with what he said and did. He made sure he treated everyone with respect and showed them how he wanted to be treated himself.

Story Thirteen – The Joke of Three Times

There once lived a wise man who loved more than anything to travel around from city to city, sharing his knowledge and helping to answer any questions people may have about life. It was his life's aim to help people.

After traveling for many years, he came upon a town where he found that everyone was always complaining about everything. Some days, the people would complain that the weather was too hot. Other days, everyone would complain that the weather was too cold. Everybody complained when there was too much sun, and they would complain whenever it rained.

Even if there were too many loaves of bread and cakes in the bakery, everyone would complain it was too hard to choose what they wanted. On the other busier days when everything had sold out, everybody would complain that there wasn't enough choice. It didn't matter what happened in the world, everybody always complained about everything.

When the wise man came to this town, he figured that they were wasting their lives complaining all the time. To help free them from this, he decided to teach them all a lesson.

One afternoon, he took a box and went to stand in the main square.

"Hear me now," the wise man exclaimed at the top of his voice and then proceeded to tell the funniest joke he could think of. The crowd never heard a joke so funny in their entire lives, and so they roared with laughter. Every single street around the square was filled with people laughing so hard, some people couldn't even stay standing up.

After calming down, the crowd waited eagerly for another joke. After a few minutes, the wise man told the same joke as he had done before. He told the joke in the same way, with the same tone of voice and enthusiasm.

Of course, having heard the joke already, a few people smiled, a few laughed, and most people stayed silent. A few minutes passed, and the wise man told the joke a third time. This time, you could only hear the hustle and bustle of the streets surrounding the main city square in which everyone was listening. No one laughed, and very few people smiled.

He spoke out loudly so everyone could hear him in a booming voice that echoed off all the walls of the surrounding buildings.

"You see, I tell the same joke three times over, and at first, it is funny, and everybody laughs. But, when I tell the joke again and again, it loses its power. The joke isn't funny anymore, and eventually, if I tell it enough times, it will mean nothing to you."

A few people nodded in agreement.

"Now look at the problems you have in your lives and complain about every single day. Yes, sometimes it's not very nice when it rains, and sometimes life doesn't go the way you want, but complaining about it over and over again doesn't make it better, just like having the good things over and over again won't make you happy."

Your words have so much power in them, like magic, so make sure you choose the right ones, and cast positive spells into the world, to help make it a nicer place for everyone.

Story Fourteen — The Gnome and the Ball

Ben had gone and lost his ball. And not just any ordinary ball. It was a bright yellow Super Shooter with red and blue stripes running down the middle, just like the one in his favorite video game. What made it even more special was that his parents had just bought it for his eight birthday.

Down a dark hole it had rolled, after he kicked it much too hard against the back garden wall. It wasn't exactly Ben's fault. He was certain the hole had not been there the day before. The grass was upturned and the hole looked like it went down and down, further and further away into a never ending dark place.

He looked around in search of help. His father was out and his mother was napping. The only things out there were a rosy-cheeked gnome and an ugly stone frog by the garden's fake pond.

"I wish there was someone to help me reach in. My arms are much too short and I'm afraid of the dark."

To Ben's surprise, the garden gnome stirred, and the stone frog turned too.

"Why do you look so sad, young man?" the garden gnome asked.

"Didn't you see?" the stone frog sighed. "He's lost his bright yellow plaything."

"Ah, perhaps there's something we can do," the garden gnome offered as Ben kept on staring. "Speak up, boy, haven't you ever been offered help before?"

But Ben was far too stunned to respond. He'd never seen a garden gnome talk, or a stone frog that chattered.

"I think he's in shock," the stone frog declared. "Perhaps it's best if we go back to rest."

"Wait, don't go!" Ben cried as he found his voice. "I've lost my ball, and I don't know how to get it back."

"Aha, a round plaything," the garden gnome replied, "you should have said so before. Those go missing quite a lot, you know. I've tracked a few lost things over the years."

Ben jumped for joy, all was not lost. He'd have his ball back and get back to playing.

"It fell down that dark hole, and I can't quite see down it." Ben pointed over to show the gnome and stone frog the small hole.

The gnome eyed the hole, and the stone frog hopped beside it. They whispered in secret and nodded in silence.

"There's no need to worry," the gnome assured him, "it's the perfect size for my body to fit in. And I have no fear for the darkness inside it. I'll pop in and grab your precious round plaything, but you ought to know nothing in life comes for free. I'll trade you a treasure for finding your ball."

Ben thought long and hard, he must have some treasure. But all he could think of was his bright yellow ball. Nothing else could compare to this one thing at all.

"I have nothing to trade with. Will my thanks be enough?" Ben hoped the rosy-cheeked gnome would spare him this kindness.

"What about that nice locket that hangs from your neck?"

Ben looked down at the object, an old gift from grandma. She'd placed it in his crib to mark his first birthday. He never really gave it much thought because it had always been there. It reminded him of grandma even when she wasn't there. Inside was a photo of Ben and grandma beside him.

"I can't trade this locket," Ben's hand wrapped firmly around it. "It's my grandma's gift."

The gnome grunted. "It's just some old metal, the ball is much newer and nicer, and must be far more special. Think of all the fun games you can play with the ball."

The stone frog raised his short hand. "But grandmas are special, he'll have to think hard."

"His grandma is old, I'm sure she won't mind. I'm sorry, young boy, it's that or the ball."

Ben pondered, and looked down the dark hole. He pictured his grandma, all sweet as she smiled. Then he pictured himself with his bright yellow ball. He had to choose now. His toy or his love?

"No, I can't give grandma's gift away for a ball. My love for my grandma is much stronger than a toy."

"Suit yourself," the garden gnome huffed. "I guess you'll never see your plaything ever again. Alright, Mr. Frog, our job here is done."

And just as they'd awoken, the gnome and stone frog turned to statues. They said nothing more when Ben tried to call them.

With no ball in hand, Ben's eyes welled up fast. He hung his head low as he went back inside. He waited in silence and tried not to cry. He was sure his parents would be mad when they heard what he'd lost.

Hours went by and his father came home. Ben ran to the door to tell him his woes, but his eyes went quite wide when he saw what he held. Right under Dad's arms was a bright yellow ball.

"My Super Shooter!" Ben yelled as he rushed to his father.

His father smiled as he dusted the ball. "Mr. Dawson found your ball by a hole in his back garden. He thinks it must have rolled through one of the holes the moles keep on digging."

Ben was so happy as he reached for the ball. But as he looked on, he saw it was filthy and quite scratched up. Because of the dirt, the yellow color was dull, and the red and blue stripes didn't look so special at all.

Ben realized right then that even though it had been shiny and new, with time, the bright yellow ball would have lost all of its glow. He smiled and placed his hand on his grandma's small locket. He was really glad he'd chosen what had truly mattered.

Final Thoughts

Once again, I just want to thank you for taking the time to read these stories. I hope they have enlightened you somehow, or at least made you think a little differently about the way life can be lived.

As a kid, your imagination is wilder and more untamed than it will be in your entire life, so try not to lose this amazing gift that you have. Tell these stories over and over again; tell them again in your own way. Perform a play in your living room while acting the stories out.

Do whatever you want; just hold onto that beautiful spark of energy you have inside you. You are strong. You are confident. You are a gift to this planet, and no one else can tell you otherwise. Even if people try to bring you down, just remember it's not true. You are perfect just the way you are.

Now go out into the world. Dream big. Create things. Meet people. Enjoy life with a smile on your face!

Disclaimer

This book contains opinions and ideas of the author and is meant to teach the reader informative and helpful knowledge while due care should be taken by the user in the application of the information provided. The instructions and strategies are possibly not right for every reader and there is no guarantee that they work for everyone. Using this book and implementing the information/recipes therein contained is explicitly your own responsibility and risk. This work with all its contents, does not guarantee correctness, completion, quality or correctness of the provided information. Misinformation or misprints cannot be completely eliminated.